The Toytown Helps Out

Story by Jenny Giles
Illustrations by Richard Hoit

Rigby®

A Harcourt Achieve Imprint

www.Rigby.com
1-800-531-5015

"I can see some smoke!"
said the Toytown bus.

3

"I can see a fire
at the farmhouse!"
said the bus.
"I will get the fire engine
to come!"

"Help, Fire Engine! Help!

I can see a fire!"

said the bus.

"Go up the hill

to the farmhouse."

"I'm on my way!"

said the fire engine.

The fire engine went
up the hill
to the farmhouse.

"Look at the smoke!"
said the fire engine.
"The farmhouse is on fire!"

"No," said the bus,
"the fire is in the garden.
Go into the yard!"

The fire engine went
into the yard.

Whoosh! Whoosh! Whoosh!

The water went onto the fire.

"The fire is out!"

shouted the fire engine.

"Oh good!" said the bus.

"The farmhouse is safe!"